Makena!
I Love you very
very much! G.ma/M?
11/17/15

Makana Aloha
Gift of Love

Written and Illustrated
by
Barbara S. McDonagh

Liko
PUBLISHING
Kealakekua, Hawaii

Makana Aloha • *Gift of Love* © 1993 by Barbara S.
McDonagh. Printed and bound in Minneapolis,
Minnesota. No part of this book may be reproduced in
any form or by any electronic or mechanical means
including information storage and retrieval systems
without permission in writing from the publisher,
except by a reviewer, who may quote brief passages in
a review. Published by Liko Publishing, P.O Box 673,
Kealakekua, Hawaii 96750. First Edition.

Library of Congress Cataloging in Publication Data

McDonagh, Barbara S.
Makana Aloha • *Gift of Love*
Summary: A lonely little girl finds a true friend who
teaches her many things about life and the sea.

ISBN 0-9643781-0-8

Acknowledgments

Two individuals came into my life and, together with my own talents and yearnings, caused the germination, growth and completion of this labor of love.

On hearing that I had written and illustrated a children's book that had been well received locally, Maxine George offered her skills as a typographer, graphic artist and editor, transforming my manuscript into a real book. Her time, encouragement and belief in this endeavor was given with pure aloha and, more than once, as I tried to find the words to thank her for taking on this work load, she said she enjoyed helping others fulfill their dreams. When asked how I could ever repay her, she told me to help someone else someday. I will try.

Without Kahu Harold H.P. Teves' friendship and nurturing, there would be no story. Aside from his capacity as unofficial literary and artistic editor, he held the key to many truths about Hawaii and life in general. He opened the door wide, ushering me into a world of knowledge about the sea and the culture of his people. Indeed, this story is the first fruit of a precious friendship, and it is only the beginning!

Me ke aloha pumehana. Mahalo nui loa.

Alphabetical glossary of Hawaiian Words:

'A'a *(Ah-ah)* — *rough, jagged lava rock*

'Ae *(Eye)* — yes

Aloha *(Ah-low-ha)* — greeting; love

Hale *(Hah-lay)* — house

Holoholo *(Hoh-low-hoh-low)* — to go out for pleasure; walk around. *(It is a tradition for an Hawaiian fisherman not to confess his intent to go fishing so that the shark will not hear of it and lay in wait for him.)*

Kamali'i *(Kah-mah-lee-ee)* — children

Keiki *(Kay-key)* — child

Kekai *(Kay-kye)* — The Sea

Koa wood *(Coe-ah)* — the largest of native forest trees; deep brown in color and only found in the Hawaiian Islands

Kupuna *(Ku-pu-nah)* — elders

Lava *(Lah-vah)* — volcanic rock

Lei po'o *(Lay poh-oh)* — floral head wreath

Liko *(Lee-coe)* — New Leaf

Limu *(Lee-moo)* — sea weed

Mahalo *(Mah-ha-low)* — thank you

Makana Aloha *(Mah-kah-nah Ah-low-ha)* — gift of friendship, gift of love

Malihini *(Mah-lee-hee-knee)* — newcomer, stranger

Mele *(Meh-lay)* — song

Napo'opo'o *(Nah-poe-oh, poe-oh)* — a little Hawaiian fishing village on the island of Hawaii, also known as the "Big Island"

Ohana *(Oh-hah-nah)* — family, relative, kin

Opihi *(Oh-pea-he)* — shell fish

Puka shell *(Poo-kah)* — a shell that has a hole in the center.

'Uo'uo *(Oo-woe-woe)* — type of mullet

Upena-ho'olei *(Oo-pen-ah hoh-oh-lay)* — throw net

Wahine *(Wah-he-nay)* — female

Dedication

To the *Kamali'i*,
learn what the *Kupuna* has to teach you.

And to my Father, Louis B. Stein,
who gave me his love for the sea,
and always told me I should write.

Makana Aloha
Gift of Love

A lonely *keiki malihini* went down to the ocean one day. The sun was warm and the sky was so blue. The ocean was crystal clear and smooth as glass. It was a beautiful Hawaiian morning!

But little Keiki *Wahine* felt very sad because everyone had someone to play with and talk to—everyone, that is, except her. She knew no one and had been taught never to speak to strangers. But here, in this beautiful bay, in this tiny village of *Napo'opo'o*, she was the stranger. With so many people on the beach and in the water, no one even smiled at her or said "*Aloha*." Perhaps, she thought, I have become invisible.

Her attention was captured by an old man walking along the ocean's edge. He was deep brown in color, like the native *koa* wood. Days in the sunshine had made him this way, and the ways of the ocean life had kept him strong. He moved purposefully from rock to rock; so quickly and nimbly, it seemed to Keiki Wahine, that he was dancing upon the *lava* rock.

Her attention was captured by an old man walking along the ocean's edge.

*H*is eyes never left the ocean. Keiki Wahine understood! He was searching the sea for fish! And the bundle he carried on his left shoulder was a net! Despite her feeling of isolation, Keiki Wahine found herself following Old Man to see what he would do.

He moved so quickly along the shoreline, she could barely keep him in sight. It required her utmost ability to keep up with him, because the *'a'a* was brittle and jagged. This caused Keiki Wahine to walk very carefully.

All of a sudden, Old Man was poised on a small ledge above the ocean. He gathered up his bundle of blue net, leaned forward, and went completely still!

Keiki Wahine froze also. As the moments passed and the waves crashed, she felt his excitement building and his love for the sea. He waited with what seemed like infinite patience, and then, with one mighty throw, he cast his net upon the water! Keiki Wahine heard it sing, "WHOOOSH" through the air, as it opened into a beautiful circle! For a split second, it hung in mid air. Then, it disappeared into the water. Old Man leaned forward, as though his very being had flown with the net, into the sea.

Old Man leaned forward, as though his very being had flown with the net, into the sea.

The next moment, he let out a "Whoop!" of triumph, and the little girl exclaimed, "Oh, wow!" The net was writhing with flapping fins and silvery bodies that glistened as the sunshine caught them! Old Man leapt into the water and carefully began to gather up his net. He first noticed Keiki Wahine as she ran down to get a closer look.

She could not contain her excitement! She called to him, "Oh! Look at all the fish you've caught!" She was surprised at the sound of joy that she heard in her own voice.

" *'Ae*," Old Man said, smiling, as he made his way out of the water carrying the net close against his chest, filled with sleek, silvery fish. "Aloha. My name is *Kekai*, The Sea. What are you called?"

"I do not know," Keiki Wahine said, shrinking back into herself. Yet she was fascinated by Kekai and his fish and could not bring herself to turn away!

"Oh! Look at all the fish you've caught!" she called, surprised at the sound of joy that she heard in her own voice.

*n*o matter. See my fish?" Kekai said, gently. Keiki Wahine nodded. She watched their struggle and could hear them screaming at him for mercy. Kekai stood over them and said, "I have caught you for a hungry family. Will you give up your life so the *ohana* can be fed?" Suddenly, the fish lay quietly in his net. They spoke with one voice and said, "We will offer ourselves as a sacrifice so that the family can be fed. We will strengthen them and give them hope, also."

Keiki Wahine helped Kekai count the fish. There were 38! He told Keiki Wahine that their name was called "*uo'uo.*"

He told Keiki Wahine that their name was called "uo'uo."

*H*e did not mind her being there. In fact, he seemed pleased. Kekai allowed her to help him carry the fish up to his little hale on the beach. She felt greatly honored. After putting the fish on ice, he said, eyes twinkling, "Let us go *holoholo* along the ocean's edge and I will share some of her secrets with you, my little friend."

Keiki Wahine felt as though Kekai was a net, surrounding her with so much aloha! She completely forgot to be sad and lonely and frightened of strangers. She listened quietly and with great attention as Kekai offered her treasures from his long life—treasures for her to hear, to understand, and to learn by.

He told her about his throw net, the *upena-ho'olei*; how he had sewn it himself, and, as a young boy, an old man had taught him to make and repair it. The old man taught him how to catch fish with his net, so he would never go hungry.

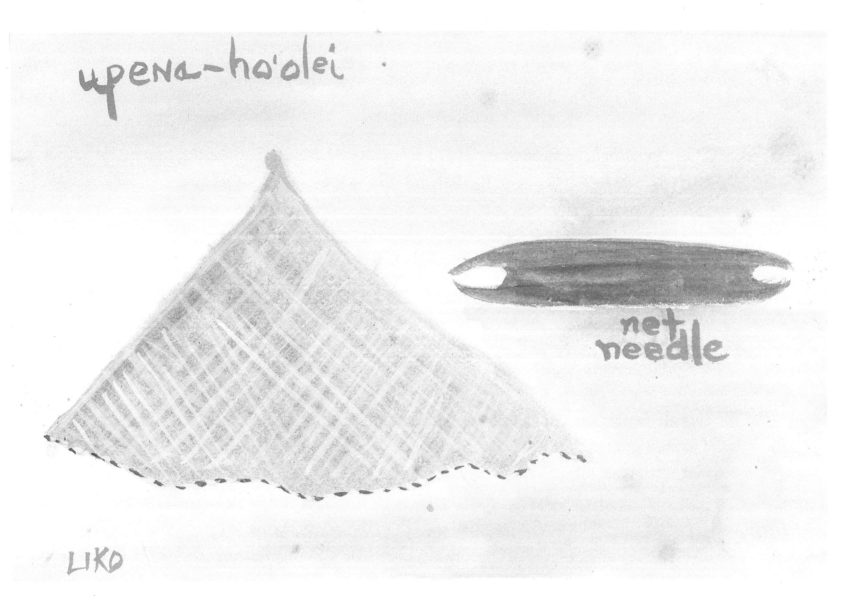

upena-ho'olei

net needle

LIKO

He told her about his throw net, the upena-ho'olei; how he had sewn it himself, and, as young boy, an old man had taught him to make and repair it. The old man taught him how to catch fish with his net, so he would never go hungry.

*H*e told her the throw-net fisherman must stand a little above the water. This is how he can see the fish and throw the upena-ho'olei so that it will open properly. Kekai pointed out, as they walked, places where fresh water came into the sea. He knew by the type of *limu* that was growing on the rocks! He showed her places he could throw his net where the bottom was relatively shallow and sandy. "Throwing net where there is coral will tear it up," he explained.

"I must think out every move I make so the fish will not see my shadow, or even the net as I throw it! In an instant the school of fish will disappear out of sight and my net will land empty."

Kekai looked solemnly at Keiki Wahine. "You must know the sea. The waves always come in sets of ten. I count them and wait until the eighth wave, when the surf is pounding and a heavy foam masks the darkness of my shadow. Then I cast my net, throwing 'blind.' When the last set breaks, I leap in after it, just like you watched me do this morning. I feel the waves. If they feel like they go through me, the feeling is good! If they try to push me back, the sea is telling me to be very careful. And I never, ever, turn my back on her. The ocean is our friend, but we must always show her great respect!"

"You must know the sea...The ocean is our friend, but we must always show her great respect!"

*K*ekai smiled gently, and the re-enactment of generations and the secrets of the sea, shone with tenderness in his eyes. He picked up a tiny *puka* shell, beautifully white and round, and held it out to Keiki Wahine. "*Mahalo*," was all she could say. She could not find the words to thank him for his time and how he gave of himself, even to her—a stranger.

Before the day said goodbye, they had walked far from Kekai's hale and back again. He showed her how to pick *opihi* and limu, and how to harvest salt by skimming the top off of the ocean filled lava pools. All this knowledge he shared with her, as they walked along the seashore!

Kekai was humming a lovely *mele* as they walked along. Keiki Wahine did not know how exactly, but she knew this day, with Old Man, had changed her life forever. This day, which had started with her feeling so empty, was ending with her being so filled. She felt her heart could not hold any more aloha!

Before the day said goodbye, they had walked far from Kekai's hale and back again.

Kekai and Keiki Wahine sat together as the beauty of the mauve sky showered them at sunset. The ocean reflected the sky, magnifying its beauty.

"Isn't it beautiful!" said Kekai.

"Yes," said Keiki Wahine.

"I have found a name for you," said Kekai. "It is 'Liko,' meaning New Leaf, because it brings new life, new knowledge, new growth. Liko! That is what I shall call you."

"Oh, mahalo, Kekai!" Liko! She loved her name. She remembered the liko she picked from the forest to make *lei po'o*, how unique and beautiful every bud was!

"*Aloha, ahiahi, Kekai. Good evening.*"

"*Aloha, Liko. Iehowa 'oe e ho'omaika'i mai, a e malama mai. The Lord bless you and keep you.*"

Kekai and Keiki Wahine sat together as the beauty of the mauve sky showered them at sunset.

About the Author

Born in New York City to elderly parents, Barbara Susan McDonagh was an only child. She grew up loving the Atlantic Ocean, but the only fish she ever saw was tuna in a can. In her wildest dreams, she never imagined the untapped bounty of the sea.

Ms. McDonagh moved out west in 1973, living in Oregon and British Columbia before coming to Hawaii in 1989. Here she was befriended by an old Hawaiian man who graciously and joyfully shared his accumulated knowledge with her. Often, he would say, "This is exactly the way we teach children about these things."

Stirred by her love for the sea and her friend's need to pass on his knowledge, she became his devoted student, sharing in each experience with him. This story recounts the beginning of a friendship that has changed her life forever. It is helping to heal a lonely little girl, and it is a *Makana Aloha* from the author to the little child in each of us.

Ms. McDonagh is a teacher in Kona and is busy putting the finishing touches on a sequel to this story. It is entitled *Na Momi Ho'omana'o, Pearls to Remember.*